This Book Belong to:

Made in the USA
Monee, IL
13 May 2024

259074cd-72b4-4a6d-bbe9-d0fafefe83e2R01